THIS BOOK BELONGS TO

....

CINDERELLA

Written by Helen Anderton
Illustrated by Stuart Lynch

make
believe
ideas

Reading together

This book is designed to be fun for children who are learning to read. The simple sentences avoid abbreviations and are written in the present tense. The big type also helps children with their word-shape recognition.

Take some time to discuss the story with your child. Here are some ways you can help your child take those first steps in reading:

❋ Encourage your child to look at the pictures and talk about what is happening in the story.

❋ Help your child to find familiar words.

❋ Ask your child to read and repeat each short sentence.

❋ Try using some of the following questions as you go along:
  • What do you think will happen next?
  • Do you like this character?
  • What kind of voice would this character have?

Sound out the words

Encourage your child to sound out the letters in any words he or she doesn't know. Look at the key words listed at the back of the book and see which of them your child can find on each page.

Reading activities

The **What happens next?** activity encourages your child to retell the story and point to the mixed-up pictures in the right order.

The **Rhyming words** activity takes six words from the story and asks your child to read and find other words that rhyme with them.

The **Key words** pages provide practice with common words used in the context of the book. Read the sentences with your child and encourage him or her to make up more sentences using the key words listed around the border.

A **Picture dictionary** page asks children to focus closely on nine words from the story. Encourage your child to look carefully at each word, cover it with his or her hand, write it on a separate piece of paper, and finally, check it!

Do not complete all the activities at once – doing one each time you read will ensure that your child continues to enjoy the story and the time you are spending together. Have fun!

Cinderella is a sweet girl.
Her mean sisters lock
her in a cellar.

The sisters receive an invite to Prince Billy's special ball.

The sisters tell Cinderella
she cannot go to the ball.

They powder their chins
and leave her behind.

A zucchini fairy appears!
She has magic green tools.

She gives Cinderella a new dress and glass shoes.

Cinderella goes to the
ball in a limousine made
of zucchini. She has to
be home by midnight.

13

Cinderella meets Prince Billy.
He is hungry.

Cinderella and the prince
eat the zucchini limousine!

Cinderella and Billy dance.
The clock strikes midnight.

Cinderella rushes home.
She leaves one shoe behind.

Billy looks for Cinderella.
Other girls try on the shoe.

They use soap and glue
but the shoe does not fit.

The sisters try on the shoe
but it does not fit them.

Cinderella hears Billy
from the cellar.

She smashes the other
shoe on a rock and
uses it to open the lock!

HOME

23

Cinderella tries on
the shoe and it fits.

Cinderella and Billy get married!

What happens next?

Some of the pictures from the story have been mixed up! Can you retell the story and point to each picture in the correct order?

Rhyming words

Read the words in the middle of each group and point to the other words that rhyme with them.

call

get

ball

long

small

dance

mean

green

queen

seat

cool

help

tool

pool

white

blue

foot

shoe

new

step

bin

car

chin

dress

grin

glass

rock

clock

shock

snack

Now choose a word and make up a rhyming chant!

The **new shoe** was bright **blue!**

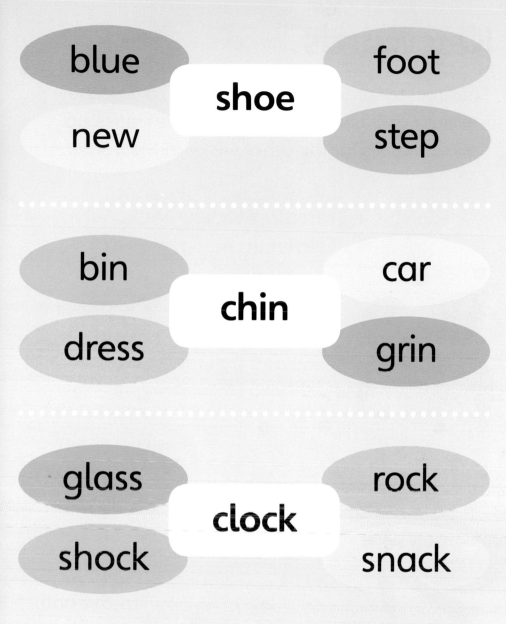

Key words

These sentences use common words to describe the story. Read the sentences and then make up new sentences for the other words in the border.

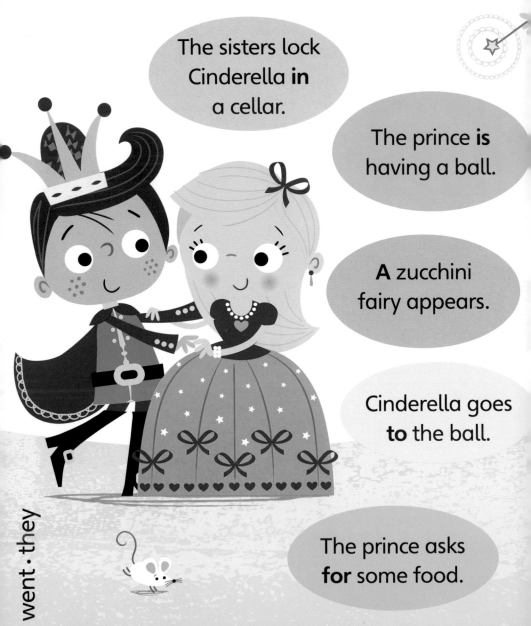

The sisters lock Cinderella **in** a cellar.

The prince **is** having a ball.

A zucchini fairy appears.

Cinderella goes **to** the ball.

The prince asks **for** some food.

went · they

· are · but · made · day · an · can · we · him · up · for ·

They eat some limousine **made** of zucchini.

Cinderella leaves **one** glass shoe behind.

The prince looks for **her**.

Cinderella tries **on** the shoe.

Cinderella marries **the** prince.

the · a · and · to · see · in · was · I · looked · he · you · of · she · on · for · when

· her · is · asked · one · at · then · have · so · be ·

Picture dictionary

Look carefully at the pictures and the words.
Now cover the words, one at a time.
Can you remember how to write them?

clock

fairy

girl

limousine

lock

prince

shoe

sister

soap